DANGEROUS GAMES

TORNADO TERROR

Sue Graves

D1188841

RISING★STARS

Rising Stars UK Ltd.
22 Grafton Street, London W1S 4EX
www.risingstars-uk.com

 **nasen**

NASEN House, 4/5 Amber Business Village, Amber Close,
Amington, Tamworth, Staffordshire B77 4RP

Text © Rising Stars UK Ltd.

The right of Sue Graves to be identified as the author of this work has
been asserted by her in accordance with the Copyright, Design and
Patents Act, 1988.

Published 2009

Cover design: pentacor**big**
Illustrations: So Creative Ltd/Calligrafic and Paul Loudon
Text design and typesetting: pentacor**big**
Publisher: Gill Budgell
Editorial project management: Lucy Poddington
Editorial consultant: Lorraine Petersen

British Library Cataloguing in Publication Data.
A CIP record for this book is available from the British Library.

ISBN: 978-1-84680-496-0

Printed by Craft Print International Limited, Singapore

CHAPTER 1

Tom had a postcard from his cousin, Luke. Luke was on a backpacking holiday in the USA with his mates from college. On the front of the card was a picture of a huge tornado spinning across the land.

Tom showed the card to Kojo and Sima. The three of them worked together at Dangerous Games, a computer games company. Sima designed the games, Kojo programmed them and Tom tested them.

"Luke and his mates have been on a storm chasing tour," explained Tom.

"What's one of those?" asked Sima.

"It's a tour where you go looking for tornadoes. You can watch the storms as they spin across the land," said Tom. "Luke says it's awesome!"

"It sounds dangerous to me," said Kojo.

"Luke says it's safe," said Tom. "The guides on the tour know what they're doing. They don't put you in any danger."

He propped the postcard against his computer. Then he looked at the picture and sighed. "I wish I was there with Luke," he said. "I'd love to go storm chasing."

Sima sat down at her desk and thought about what Tom had said. It gave her an idea. She went online and looked up information about storm chasing. She found out about a part of the USA called Tornado Alley, where there are lots of tornadoes. She made some notes. Then she went to have a chat with Tom and Kojo.

"I've got an idea for a new game," she told them.

Tom looked up from his work. "Go on," he said.

"Why don't I design a new computer game about storm chasing?" said Sima. "There's an area of the USA called Tornado Alley. Part of it is in Texas. I could set the game there. The aim would be to escape from as many tornadoes as you can before you run out of time. And best of all, we could test the game for real, like we've done before."

Tom's mouth dropped open. "Have I told you you're amazing?" he said.

Sima blushed. "Maybe once or twice," she mumbled. Then she smiled. "I take it you like my idea, then?"

"You bet," said Tom and Kojo together.

"Then I'd better get to work," she said.

Sima worked hard on the designs for the new game.

The next day, she gave them to Kojo so that he could program them onto the computer.

"It looks good, Sima," he said. "The game should be ready to test on Friday evening, if that's OK."

"Sure is," said Sima.

"This is going to be great!" said Tom.

On Friday, when everyone had gone home for the evening, Kojo started up the game.

"Let me remind you …" he began.

Sima and Tom laughed. "We know! We've all got to touch the screen at the same time to enter the game," said Sima.

"Yep," said Kojo. "And don't forget …"

"Yeah, yeah!" said Tom. "The game's only over when we hear the voice say 'Game over'. You tell us every time!"

Kojo looked hurt. "But it's important!"

Sima gave him a hug. "I know. Come on, let's get into the game."

They touched the screen together. A bright light flashed so brightly it hurt their eyes. They shut them tight.

CHAPTER 2

When Kojo, Tom and Sima opened their eyes, they were standing on a vast plain in Texas and the sun was going down. They looked around them. The plain stretched far into the distance and there was no one else around. Nearby was a large truck. It had gigantic wheels and bright orange flames were painted on its sides. On the roof was a small radar dish. The dish went round and round very slowly.

IS THAT FOR US?

"What's with the radar?" asked Kojo, pointing to the radar dish.

"That's very important," said Sima. "It will help us to track any tornadoes nearby. The radar will also show us how big the storms are. There's a screen in the truck. Come on, I'll show you."

They climbed into the truck. The radar screen was on the dashboard. Tom, Sima and Kojo watched it closely. Suddenly a red swirl appeared on one side of the screen. It was moving quickly.

DON'T BE A LOSER!

Tom patted the steering wheel. "In this beauty, we'll be able to outrun any tornado. Don't you think, Sima?"

But Sima wasn't listening. She was staring out of the window.

"Sima, did you hear me?" asked Tom.

"Here it comes," she said. She pointed across the plain. "Look!"

Tom leaned across to look out of the window. A huge black mass of cloud had appeared in the distance. The cloud was spinning fast. It was twisting across the plain ... and it was heading straight for them.

"OK, guys," said Tom. "Let's get out of here." He turned the ignition key. But the truck wouldn't start.

TRY AGAIN. WE'VE GOT TO GET OUT OF HERE FAST!

48:00

HURRY UP, TOM! THE TORNADO'S GETTING CLOSER AND CLOSER.

Tom turned the key again. The truck started. Quickly, Tom pushed the gear stick forward. The gears grated loudly and then the truck shot forward.

Tom pressed his foot down hard on the accelerator. The wheels spun as the truck picked up speed.

Kojo looked at the radar screen. The
tornado was catching up with them fast.

"You need to go much faster," he said.
"If the tornado catches up with us,
we've had it."

Tom pressed the accelerator pedal
down to the floor. The engine got
noisier and noisier. The truck sped
across the plain.

Sima held on tightly to her seat.

THE TORNADO'S CHANGING DIRECTION IT'S GOING AWAY FROM US NOW.

Tom slowed the truck down. He looked in his wing mirror. The tornado was moving away from them.

"I thought the chase would last much longer than that," he said. He was disappointed. "You'll have to improve this game a bit, Sima. Make it more exciting."

Sima sat back in her seat. "Yes, that was a bit too easy," she said.

CHAPTER 3

They drove across the plain in search of another tornado. But the radar screen stayed blank.

Tom began to play about with the truck. He made it go faster, then he swung the steering wheel round. He braked hard. The truck skidded round and round. Dust shot up in the air and fell onto the windscreen.

NICE ONE, MATE. NOW WE CAN'T SEE WHERE WE'RE GOING. WHAT IF WE HIT SOMETHING?

"There's nothing out here to hit," said Tom. "We might as well have some fun while we look for the next tornado."

He pressed the accelerator harder. Then he braked really hard. The truck spun round and round again. Sima screamed at him.

STOP IT TOM, WE'LL HAVE AN ACCIDENT!

But it was too late. Suddenly the truck smashed into a rock. The truck spun up into the air. Then it crashed down and rolled over and over. Petrol poured out from the tank and trickled along the ground.

Tom pushed the door open and climbed out. Then he helped Kojo and Sima out. They ran as fast as they could away from the truck.

There was a loud explosion behind them. The truck had burst into a ball of flames.

"Tom, you idiot, you could have killed all of us," said Kojo angrily. "What are we going to do now? We're stuck in the middle of a plain in Texas with no truck."

"It's OK," said Sima. "All we have to do is wait until the time runs out. Then we'll hear 'Game over' and we'll be back in the office again."

"Bit of a boring game, Sima," grumbled Tom. He sat down on the ground.

AND NOW IT'S GETTING DARK, TOO!

CHAPTER 4

Tom and Kojo listened. They could hear the rumble of thunder in the distance. They could hear the wind howling, too. It grew louder and louder. They looked out across the plain into the darkness. They could see a dark cloud twisting quickly towards them. Lightning flashed out of it.

IT'S A TORNADO. RUN!

They ran as fast as they could. But the tornado was getting closer and closer. Thunder boomed and lightning flashed all around them. Then large hailstones began to crash down out of the sky. The hailstones stung their backs as they ran through the storm.

Tom looked behind him. The tornado was nearly on top of them.

Kojo flung himself to the ground. He covered his head with his arms.

But Sima stood there looking at Tom. She was frozen to the spot with fear.

Tom grabbed her and pushed her to the ground. Then he threw himself down next to her. He wrapped his arms round her and held her tight.

07:00

CHAPTER 5

The storm hit them with its full force. They could feel the tornado pulling and tugging at them. The noise of the storm roared above them. Lightning struck the ground around them. They could smell burning dust as the ground caught fire.

Then suddenly the storm was gone. Everything went very quiet and still.

Tom raised his head.

IT'S GOING AWAY NOW. LOOK!

Kojo and Sima looked up and watched as the tornado whirled away from them.

It twisted over the burning truck and sucked it up into the air. They watched as the truck spun around inside the tornado. It looked like a little toy. Seconds later it dropped back to the ground and split into hundreds of pieces.

THANK GOODNESS WE WEREN'T IN THE TRUCK. WE'D ALL HAVE BEEN KILLED!

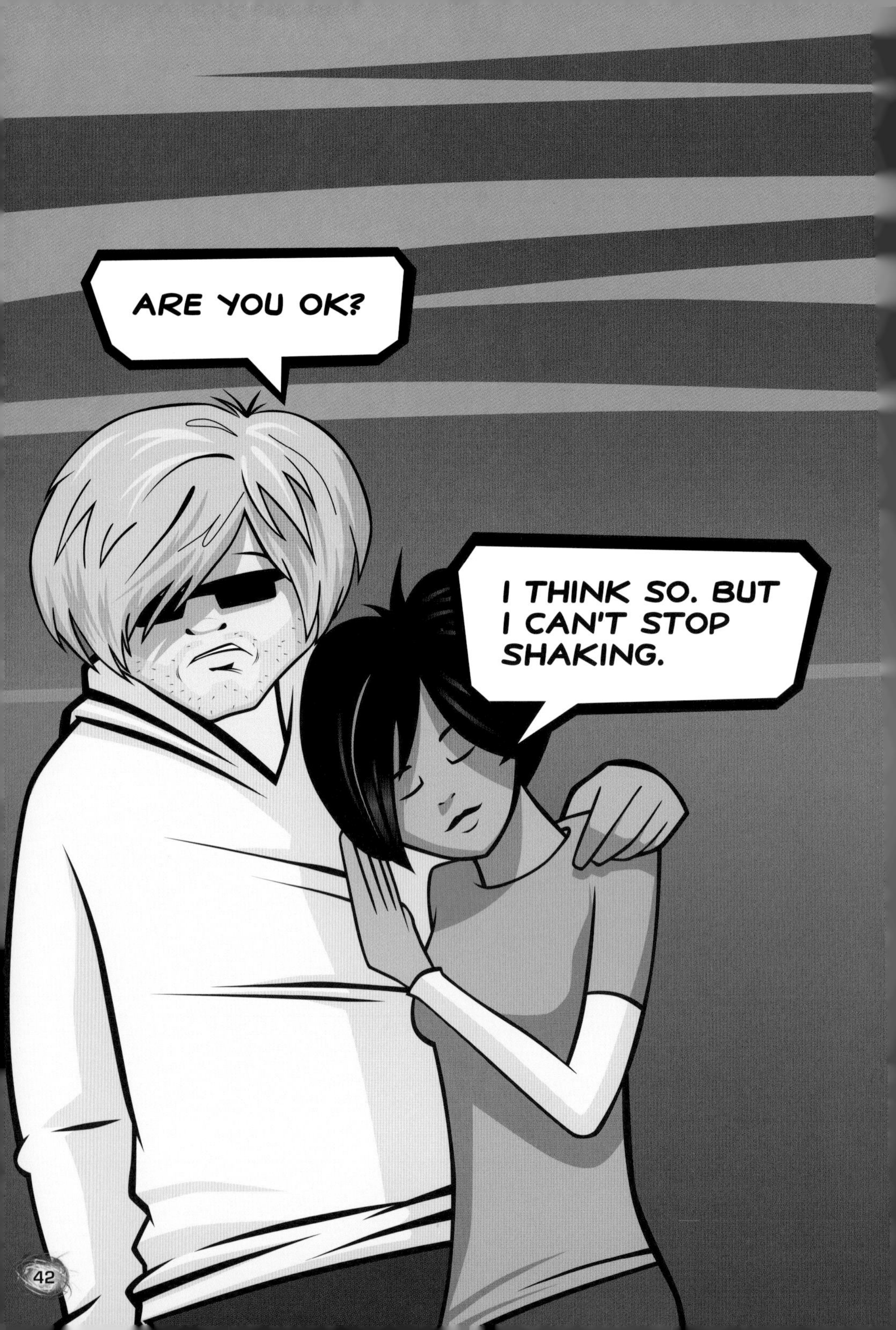
ARE YOU OK?
I THINK SO. BUT I CAN'T STOP SHAKING.

Tom stood up and helped Sima to her feet.
He put his arm round her. Sima clung onto
him and rested her head on his shoulder.

Just then they heard a loud voice saying
"Game over."

A bright light flashed, hurting their eyes.
They shut them tight.

The bright light faded. They were back in the office.

"Do you still wish you were storm chasing with your cousin, Tom?" Kojo said.

"Maybe not!" said Tom. "He's welcome to it."

He glanced down at a newspaper lying on his desk. He picked it up and grinned. "Fancy coming out with me tonight, Sima?" he said. "There's a new film on at the cinema that you might like to see."

"What's that?" asked Sima.

"Tornado Terror!" said Tom.

"Oh sure!" Sima punched him on the arm. "After all, we haven't had quite enough excitement for one day!"

Glossary of terms

dashboard the place inside a vehicle where information is displayed, such as the speed and amount of fuel in the tank

ignition key the key you use to start a vehicle's engine

plain a large area of flat land

program to write a computer game or other computer program

radar a way of finding out the position of something using radio signals

radar dish a round piece of equipment that sends or receives radio signals

tornado a strong wind that twists as it moves

wing mirror a mirror on the side of a vehicle which allows the driver to see what is happening behind it

QUIZ

1 What was the name of Tom's cousin?

2 Where was his cousin backpacking?

3 Who was his cousin with?

4 What sort of tour did Tom's cousin go on?

5 Where are there lots of tornadoes in America?

6 What was on the roof of the truck?

7 What did Tom crash into?

8 What spilled out of the truck?

9 What hit Tom, Sima and Kojo as they tried to run away from the tornado?

10 What was the name of the film Tom wanted to take Sima to see?

ABOUT THE AUTHOR

Sue Graves has taught for thirty years in Cheshire schools. She has been writing for more than ten years and has written well over a hundred books for children and young adults.

"Nearly everyone loves computer games. They are popular with all age groups – especially young adults. But I've often thought it would be amazing to play a computer game for real. To be in on the action would be the best experience ever! That's why I wrote these stories. I hope you enjoy reading them as much as I've enjoyed writing them for you."

ANSWERS TO QUIZ

1   Luke

2   In the USA

3   His mates from college

4   Storm chasing

5   Tornado Alley

6   A radar dish

7   A rock

8   Petrol

9   Hailstones

10   Tornado Terror